For information address Disney • Lucasfilm Press,
1101 Flower Street, Glendale, California 91201.

Printed in China
First Hardcover Edition, July 2016   10 9 8 7 6 5 4 3 2 1

ISBN 978-1-4847-8703-8
FAC-023680-16195

Visit the official *Star Wars* website at: www.starwars.com
This book was printed on paper created from a sustainable source.

STAR WARS

The Revelation

Disney | LUCASFILM PRESS

Los Angeles • New York

Luke Skywalker was on a mission to save his friends. The Force had sent him a vision showing that they were in trouble. Now, he was headed to Cloud City to help.

As Luke's X-wing approached Cloud City, the young Jedi could sense trouble through the Force. After landing, Luke moved down the quiet hallways of the floating city.

Luke drew his blaster, and just in time. The bounty hunter Boba Fett was waiting for him. He fired on Luke, missing the young Jedi by only a few inches.

"Luke!" Princess Leia shouted. "Don't—it's a trap!"

As Luke ducked behind a wall, he caught a glimpse of his friends being led away by Imperial stormtroopers.

Luke chased after his friends and found himself in a carbon-freezing facility. The hum of electricity and a haze of steam filled the air. A deep robotic breathing echoed throughout the chamber as Darth Vader stepped from the shadows.

"The Force is with you, young Skywalker," Vader rasped, "but you are not a Jedi yet."

Luke ignited his lightsaber. It glowed with blue energy. Vader's lightsaber burned bright red. Luke thought of his former mentor, Obi-Wan Kenobi, and how he had died at Darth Vader's hands. Then he thought of his friends, whom he needed to save. There was no choice for Luke but to fight.

The red and blue lightsabers sparked as they clashed together—the duel had begun!

Elsewhere in the city, Lando Calrissian instructed his guards to free Princess Leia and Chewbacca.

"What do you think you're doing?" Leia asked as Lando released Chewbacca from his handcuffs.

But before Lando could answer, Chewie started choking him. Lando had betrayed Han. He couldn't be trusted. Or could he?

"There's still a chance to save Han," Lando gasped. "At the east platform . . ."

Not far away, Boba Fett was loading a carbonite-frozen Han Solo onto his ship. Lando, Leia, and Chewie rushed through the corridors of Cloud City to save him.

They were almost there. As the door to the platform opened, they fired their blasters . . . but it was too late. The bounty hunter's ship rose into the sky and flew away.

Lando and Leia decided headed to the *Millennium Falcon*. Maybe they could still catch Boba Fett.

Meanwhile, in the carbon-freezing facility, Vader had cornered Luke. As the young Jedi took a step back, he fell into the carbon-freezing chamber. Just as he was about to be frozen, Luke used the Force to make an impossible leap.

"Impressive," Vader said, slashing through machinery with his lightsaber. "Obi-Wan has taught you well. You have controlled your fear. Now release your anger. Only your hatred can destroy me!"

Luke refused to give in to his anger. He had learned from the Jedi Master Yoda how dangerous anger could be. But he was growing weaker every minute. He could not hold out against Vader much longer.

The Sith Lord used the Force to hurl large metal objects at Luke. The young Jedi wasn't strong enough to dodge them. He was hit again and again, until Vader pushed a large metal pipe through the window. All the air was sucked out of the room— and Luke Skywalker was taken with it!

Luke clung to a metal catwalk over the central air shaft within Cloud City. Just as he climbed up onto the catwalk, Darth Vader emerged and the battle began again.

"It is useless to resist," Vader rasped through his helmet.

Luke swung his lightsaber, but Vader was faster. In one fell swoop, Vader cut off Luke Skywalker's hand!

Luke clutched his wrist. He struggled to escape from the Sith Lord, but there was nowhere to go.

"If you only knew the power of the dark side," Vader said through his mask. "Obi-Wan never told you what happened to your father. . . ."

"He told me you killed him," Luke snapped.

"No," Darth Vader said. "I am your father."

"No!" Luke shouted. "It's not true! That's impossible!" He screamed in anguish. How could his greatest enemy turn out to be his father?

"Join me," Darth Vader said, extending his hand, "and together we can rule the galaxy as father and son."

Luke looked around. There was no escape. Either he could join his father, or he could let go.

"Come with me," Vader instructed. "It is the only way."

But Luke would not give in to the dark side. Taking one last look at Vader, he let go of the catwalk.

Luke fell down the central air shaft and into the vents that blew air throughout Cloud City. He was ejected into the sky but managed to grab hold of an antenna before he plummeted to the distant clouds below.

With nowhere left to go, Luke used the Force to reach out to Leia.

The *Millennium Falcon* was just about to break orbit when Leia felt Luke's pleas for help. "We've got to go back," Leia told Lando and Chewie.

They found Luke, barely alive, hanging from the antenna. Carefully, they moved the ship below and rescued him.

Leia made sure that Luke was secure in a medical bed, then returned to the main cabin. Lando and Chewie were trying to make the jump to lightspeed, but the hyperdrive still wasn't responding. They were sitting ducks as a giant Star Destroyer appeared.

Vader sensed that Luke was on board. He commanded his men to grab the ship with the Star Destroyer's tractor beam.

Chewbacca and R2-D2 desperately tried to get the hyperdrive working. Just as the Empire was about to recapture the rebels, the *Millennium Falcon* blasted off at lightspeed, escaping into hyperspace.

Later, aboard a rebel medical ship, Luke was fitted with a robotic hand to replace the one he had lost. Though Luke had gone to rescue his friends, his friends had rescued him.

Now that they had escaped Vader, it was time to rescue Han. Lando and Chewie were leaving in the *Millennium Falcon* to find the bounty hunter who had taken their friend.

"We'll find Han," Lando said. "I promise."

Luke nodded. "May the Force be with you," he said.